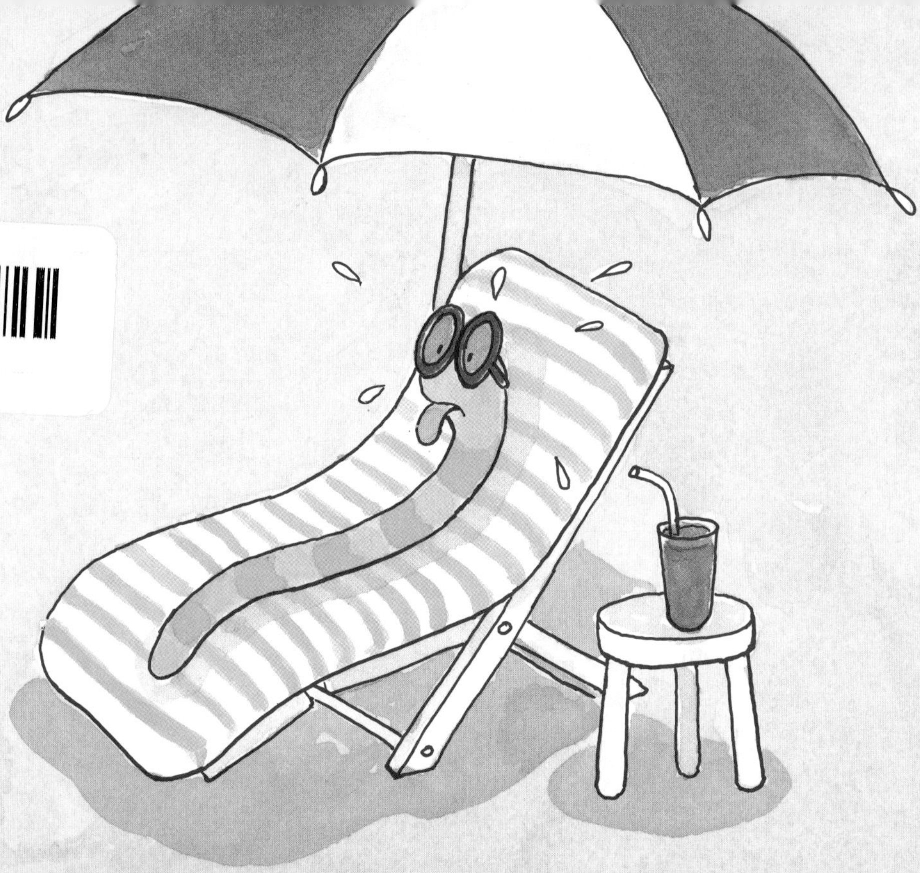

Worm is hot.

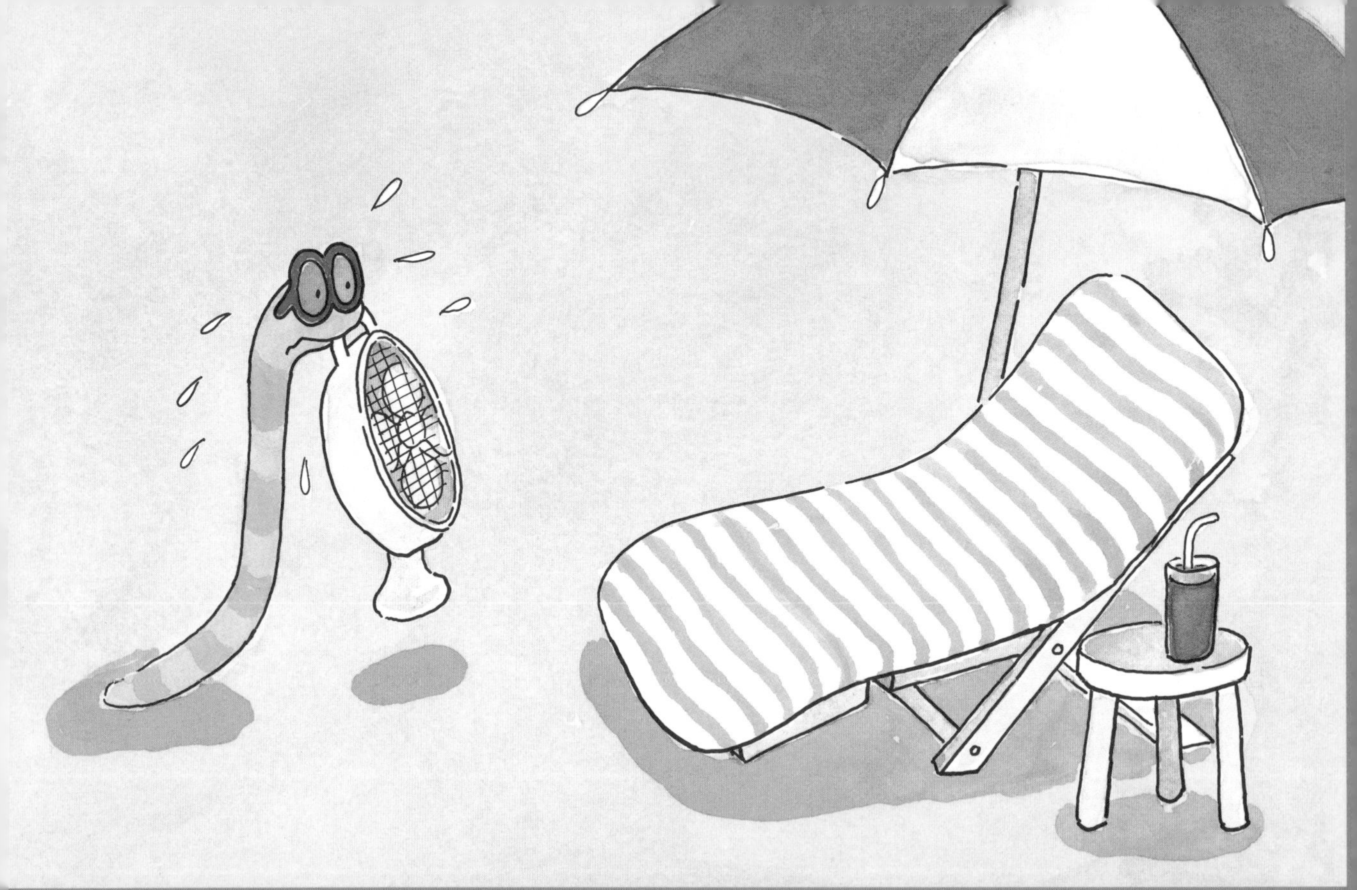

Worm gets a fan.

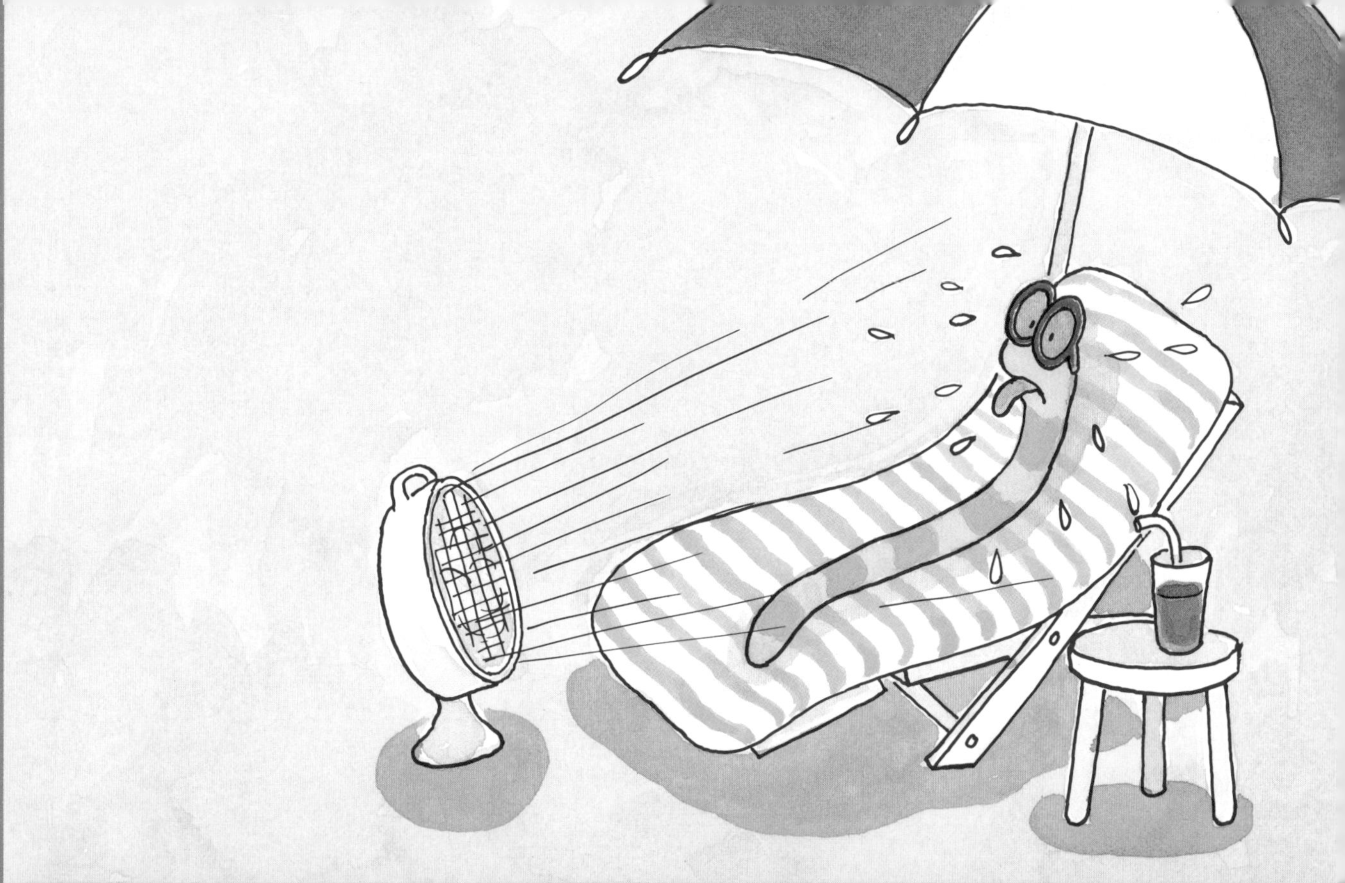

Worm is still hot.

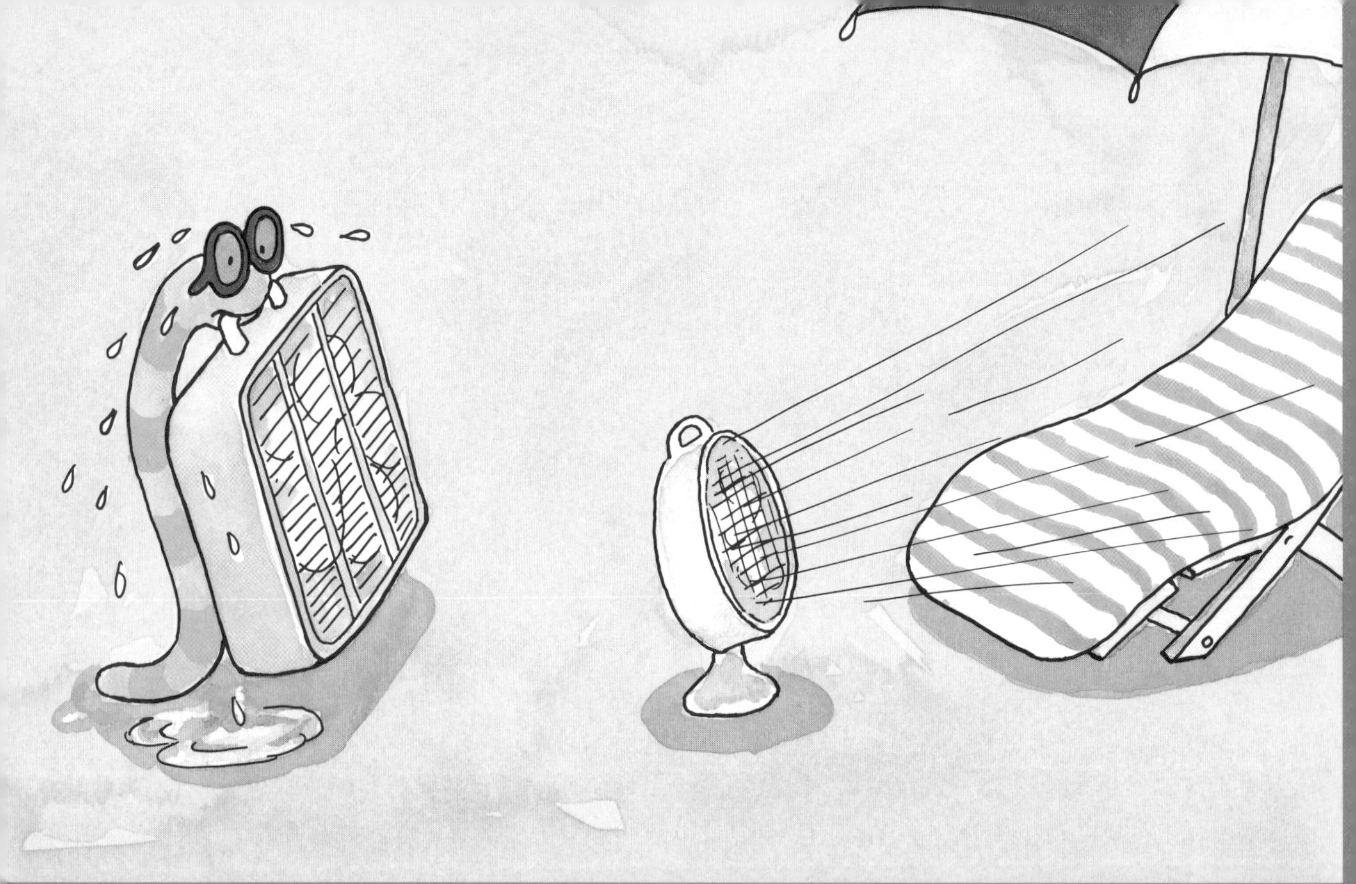

Worm gets another fan.

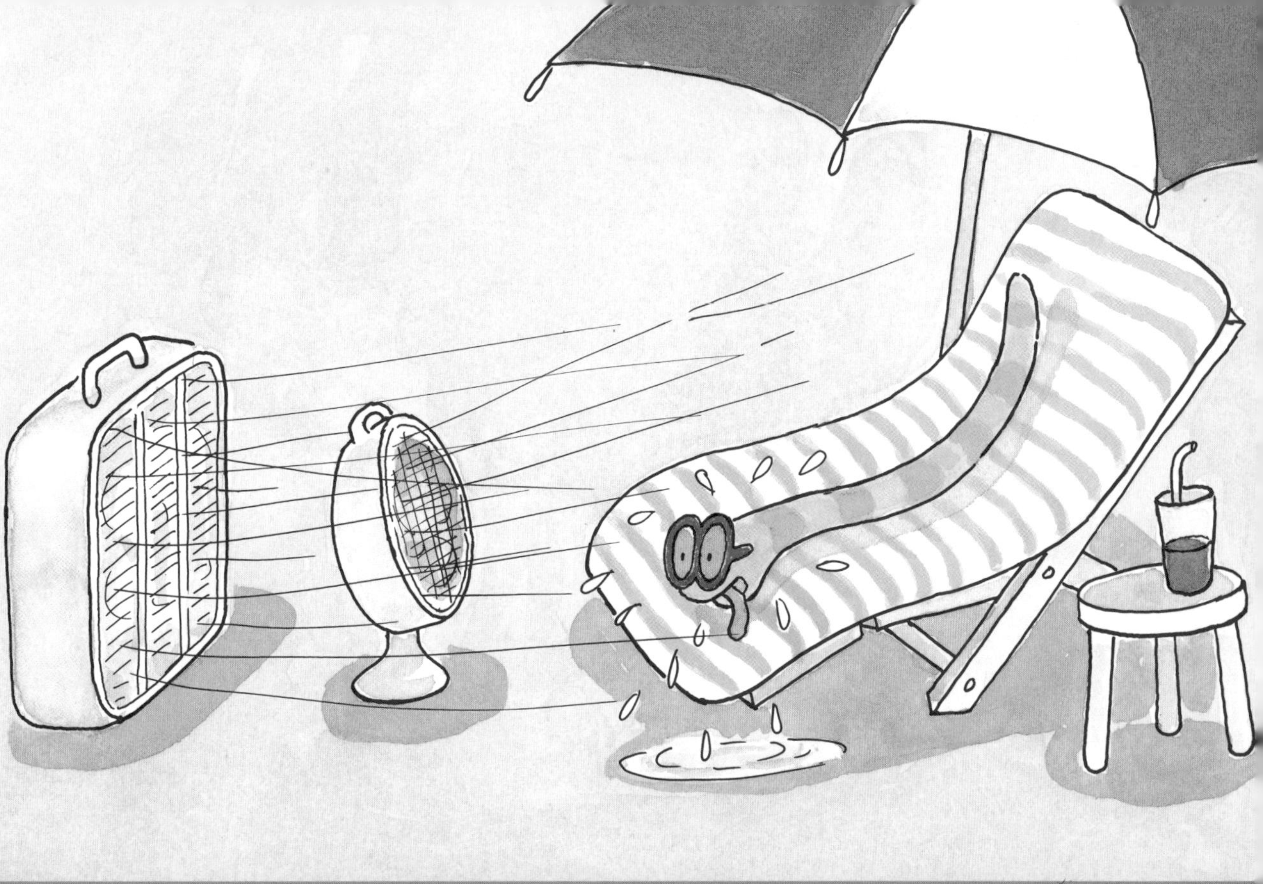

Worm is still hot.

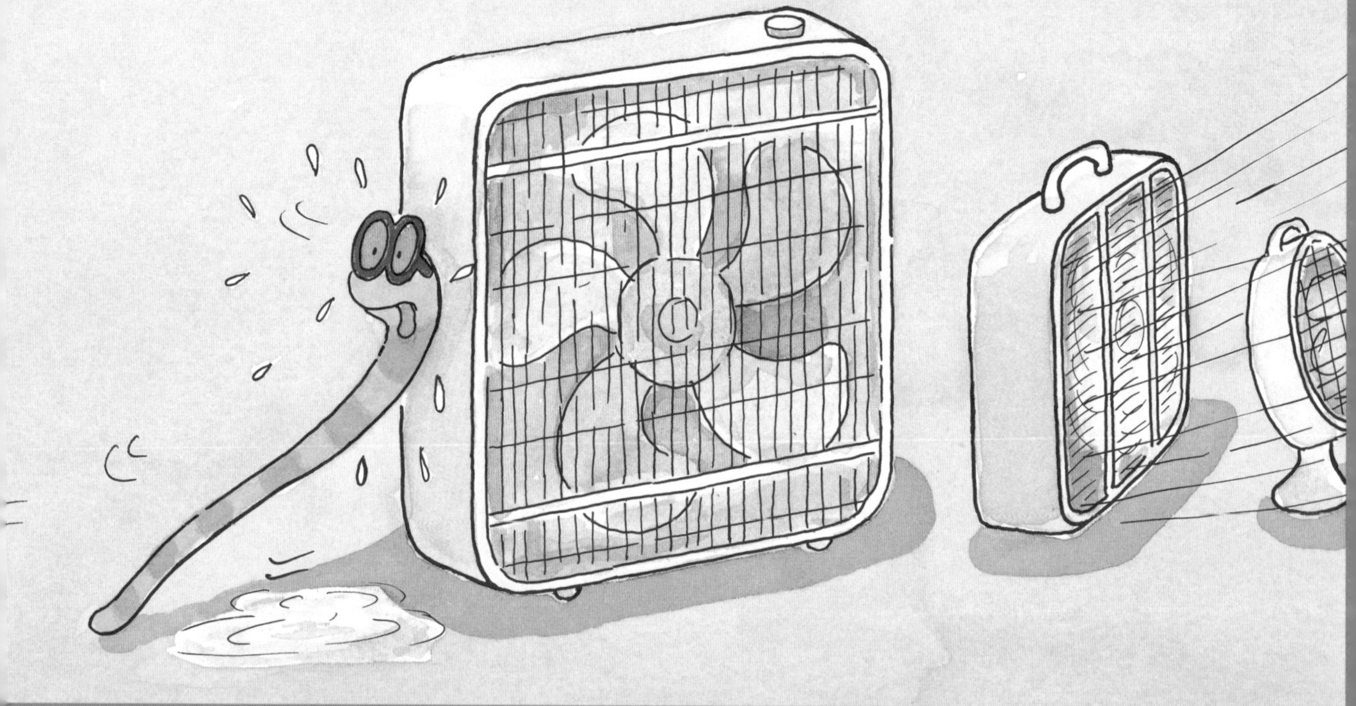

Worm gets another fan.

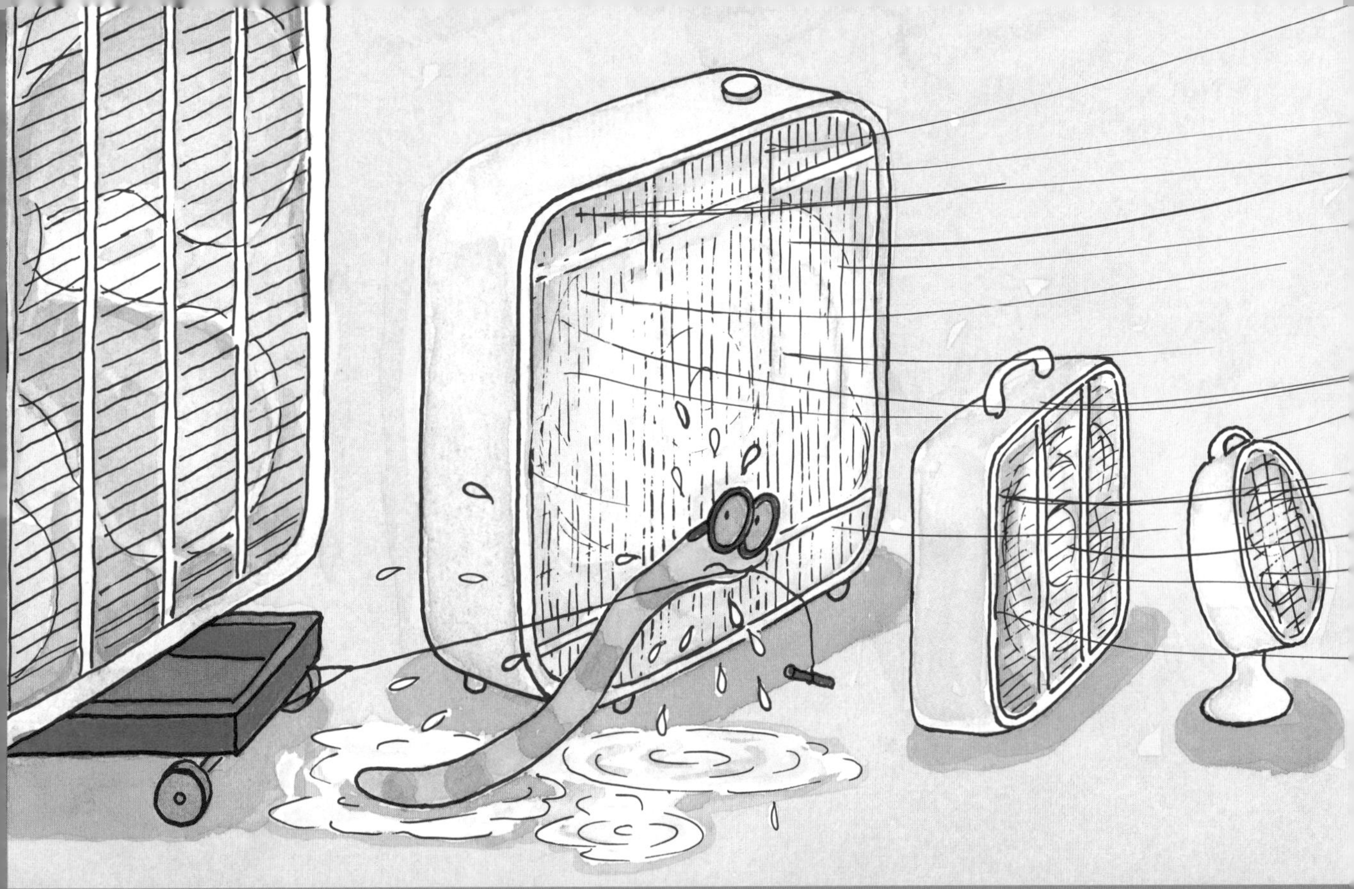

Worm gets ANOTHER fan.

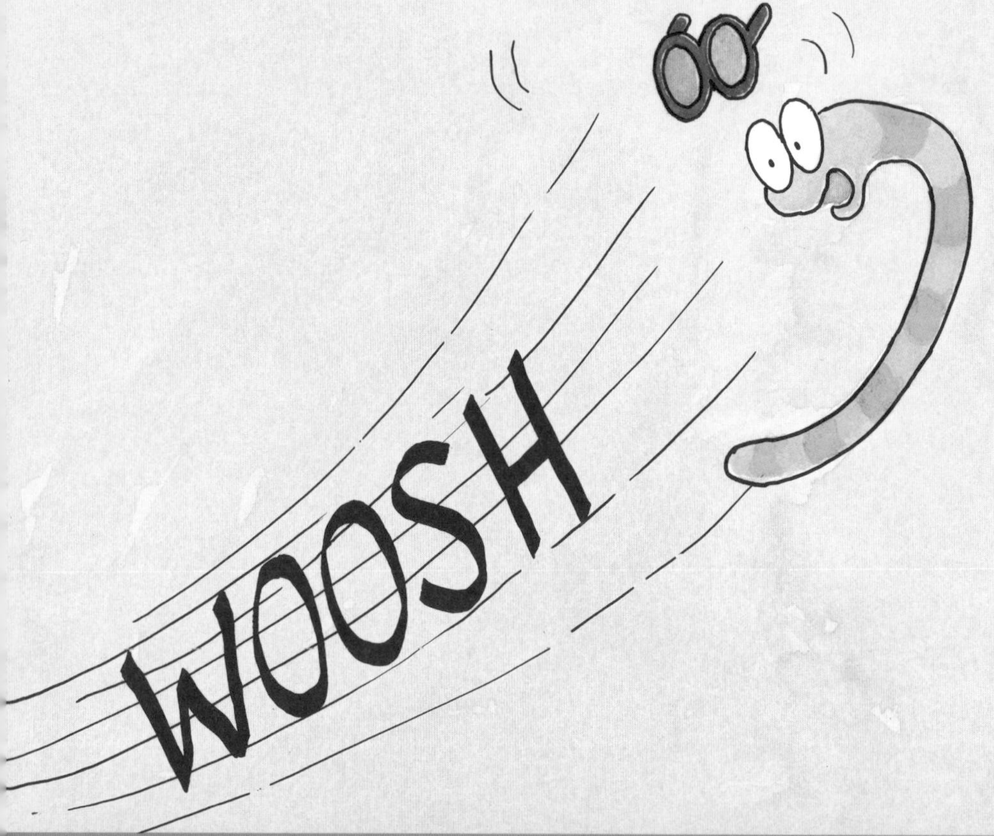

Worm blows away.